Mission: Forgiveness

A Discovery Mountain Interactive Faith Exercise

Mission: Forgiveness

A Discovery Mountain Interactive Faith Exercise

Jean Boonstra

Pacific Press®
Publishing Association

Nampa, Idaho | www.pacificpress.com

Cover design by Kyle Warren
Cover illustration by Marcus Mashburn
Inside design by Aaron Troia

The author assumes full responsibility for the accuracy of all facts
and quotations as cited in this book.

Bible quotations are from the New King James Version®. Copyright
© 1982 by Thomas Nelson. Used by permission. All rights reserved.

Purchase additional copies of this book by calling toll-free
1-800-765-6955 or by visiting AdventistBookCenter.com.

Library of Congress Cataloging-in-Publication Data

Names: Boonstra, Jean Elizabeth, author.
Title: Mission: forgiveness : an interactive Discovery Mountain
    faith exercise / Jean Boonstra.
Description: Nampa, Idaho : Pacific Press Publishing Association,
    2020. | Audience: Ages 9-12. | Summary: Invites the reader to
    make a series of choices as a new student in Chaplain Jake's
    class at Discovery Mountain Academy, who accidentally injures
    another student then seeks forgiveness.
Identifiers: LCCN 2020001417 | ISBN 9780816366521 (paperback)
    | ISBN 9780816366538 (Kindle edition)
Subjects: LCSH: Plot-your-own stories. | CYAC: Forgiveness—Fiction.
    | Christian life—Fiction. | Accidents—Fiction. | Plot-your-own
    stories.
Classification: LCC PZ7.B64613 Ml 2020 | DDC [Fic]—dc23
LC record available at https://lccn.loc.gov/2020001417

March 2020

Introduction

There is nowhere in the world like Discovery Mountain. Mr. Simon founded the small town in 1968 when he landed his plane, Blue Birdie, in the picturesque mountain valley. Mr. Simon believes that God sends just the right people to Discovery Mountain—and it's true! One day Jacob P. Donovan—better known as Jake—thought that he was running away from God. Instead, God sent Jake to Discovery Mountain, and he became a chaplain and Bible teacher.

God sent Jamey to Discovery Mountain too! She's Mr. Simon's granddaughter. Jamey and Kayla will help you with your mission—listen to their advice. God sent Harold Peabody to town, too, when his dad became the church pastor. God called Logan Lewis away to the mission field and then sent him right back to Discovery Mountain.

6

God sent Lana, Gracie, Judah, Miss Michelle, Natasha, and, well, you get the idea. God sends just the right people to this special small town. You're on your way there, you'll see what I mean!

—Ms. Jean

PS Listeners visit Discovery Mountain each week through the podcast program *Discovery Mountain*. If you've never listened to the program start with the introductory mini adventure found at DiscoveryMountain.com/welcome and meet the characters who will help (or hinder) you on your mission.

Preface

Have you ever wondered what it would be like to visit Discovery Mountain? Could you exercise your faith if you were put to the test? Would you make the right choices if you were challenged?

If you're ready to apply your faith, I challenge you to turn the page. Inside you'll find your first Discovery Mountain faith exercise. It begins in Chaplain Jake's Bible classroom. Where will it end? That's up to you! With the help of your favorite characters, you choose what happens next. Will you follow their advice (warning—they might not always be right) and find forgiveness? Or will you choose a different path? What will the consequences be? Will you leave with your faith strengthened? Or will you leave Discovery Mountain weaker than when you started?

Remember, you can always turn the pages back

and make a different choice. If you're ready, turn the page!

—Ms. Jean

PS Warning—keep your eyes open for the plant thief, and you might spot her!

R *ing! Ring!*

You walk as quietly—and quickly—as you can down the hall. You heard the bell ring, but you couldn't find the classroom. This is your first visit to Discovery Mountain Academy. Maybe Chaplain Jake won't hear you come in late. Carefully, you open the classroom door.

"You're late," Chaplain Jake says with a questioning tone. The class turns and looks at you, and you feel your cheeks flush red with embarrassment. Pointing to the empty desk in the front row, Chaplain Jake motions you into the classroom. You walk to the front and nervously tuck your legs under the chair.

"Do you belong in this class?" Chaplain Jake asks. He's trying to remember if he's seen you before.

"I'm visiting," you answer.

Chaplain Jake nods—he accepts your presence.

"We're reading John five," he explains to you. You reach into your coat pocket. Did you remember to bring your Bible? Your fingers touch the leather cover, and, feeling relieved, you set your Bible and multicolored pen on the desk. Quickly, you find the book of John and flip to chapter five.

"Who will read for us?" Chaplain Jake asks the class. You avoid his eyes—you don't want to draw any more attention to yourself than you already have.

"I'll read," a familiar voice says. It's Harold Peabody. You pinch yourself—this isn't a dream! You're really in class with Chaplain Jake and Harold!

Harold reads. "Now there is in Jerusalem by the Sheep Gate a pool, which is called in Hebrew, Bethesda, having five porches. In these lay a great multitude of sick people, blind, lame, paralyzed, waiting for the moving of the water" (John 5:2, 3).

You click your pen to the red color and neatly underline the word "waiting."

"There are a lot of people waiting by the pool of Bethesda. One has faith. Read verse five, Harold," Chaplain Jake says.

You turn to peek at Harold. He brushes his hair out of his eyes as he bends over his Bible. "Now a certain man was there who had an infirmity thirty-eight years" (John 5:5).

You write "thirty-eight" in red in the margin of your Bible.

"Thirty-eight years? What was his 'infirmity'?" a voice asks. She's sitting right across from you. It's Lana!

"The man had been paralyzed for thirty-eight years. But his wait was almost over," Chaplain Jake answers. "Lana, read the next verse for us."

Lana squints at her Bible and reads, "When Jesus saw him lying there, and knew that he already had been in that condition a long time, He said to him, 'Do you want to be made well?' " (John 5:6).

You underline the last part of the verse. *Did the man want to be made well?* you wonder.

"Chaplain Jake," someone asks. "Did the man want to be made well?" You glance over your shoulder—it's Logan Lewis. He just asked the very question you were thinking!

"Let's find out," Chaplain Jake answers. "Logan, read the next few verses."

You hear Logan turn the page in his Bible and

begin to read, "The sick man answered Him, 'Sir, I have no man to put me into the pool when the water is stirred up; but while I am coming, another steps down before me.' Jesus said to him, 'Rise, take up your bed and walk.' And immediately the man was made well, took up his bed, and walked" (John 5:7–9).

You underline the words "no man" and Jesus' words to the man, "Rise, take up your bed and walk." You've never read this story before—at least not like this. Jesus healed the paralyzed man! As you think about it, you draw a heart in the margin next to the verse. You don't want to forget this miracle. You're so absorbed in your thoughts that you don't hear Chaplain Jake's voice.

"What do you think?" Chaplain Jake says again, and you realize he's asking you the question.

"What do I think?" you stammer. "About which part again?"

Chaplain Jake smiles. "Did the paralyzed man have to do anything to be healed?"

You look at your Bible and the red-underlined words. You're too nervous to think clearly. "I'm not sure," you manage to say.

Chaplain Jake scrunches his eyebrows and seems to wonder if you really belong in his class-room.

"He had to believe that Jesus would heal him," Harold says.

Chaplain Jake turns to Harold. You breathe a sigh of relief. "Yes! He had to believe and stand up in faith," Chaplain Jake says, leaning over Harold's desk.

"There's another verse that I don't understand," Harold adds.

"Read it," Chaplain Jake answers.

"Afterward Jesus found him in the temple, and said to him, 'See, you have been made well. Sin no more, lest a worse thing come upon you' " (John 5:14).

You underline the words "worse thing."

"What would be worse than being paralyzed with no one to help you?" Harold asks.

"Jesus made the man physically well," Chaplain Jake answers. "He told him to 'sin no more.' Not having forgiveness for his sins would be worse."

"Worse than being paralyzed with no one to help you for thirty-eight years?" Logan asks.

"Yes! Forgiveness of sin means that we will live forever with Jesus. Missing that would be worse than lying at the pool of Bethesda for thirty-eight years," Chaplain Jake explains.

You hear the bell ring. Class is over—but you still have unanswered questions. As everyone leaves, you have an idea! You'll write your questions in your notebook—you might have a chance to ask Chaplain Jake about them later.

Standing up, you search your pockets for your notebook. You find it, but it's wedged in a small pocket. It's stuck.

"Welcome to our class," Harold greets you.

You turn to say hello to Harold, still struggling to get your notebook unstuck from your pocket. Suddenly, the notebook comes free, and you feel your arm swing out wildly. Your arm crashes into something—hard.

"*Oof*," you hear Harold say, and horrified, you realize what happened. You just accidentally hit Harold across the throat with your outstretched arm!

Gasping for breath, Harold falls to the floor. "I, I can't breathe," he croaks.

If you choose to run home before anyone realizes what you just did, turn to page 57.

If you choose to find help for Harold, turn to page 17.

You run around the corner. You see an open window at the end of the hall. You run as fast as you can and jump out of the window. Landing in the grass, you stand up and check yourself. You're all right!

"Wait!" you hear Chaplain Jake call from inside the school. You start running again, and you don't turn around.

You finally stop to catch your breath when you reach the river on the edge of town. A car pulls up and stops, so you hide behind a tree. A family exits the car and sets up a picnic lunch on the table by the river. You realize they aren't looking for you, and you relax.

Looking out at the river, you think about the verse that Harold shared with you, Matthew 7:7. "Ask, and it will be given to you; seek, and you will find; knock, and it will be opened to you."

You wish that you could ask God for forgiveness. You want to.

You watch the family enjoy their lunch.

Opening your notebook, you write these words: "God's forgiveness is free if you *ask* for it."

Then you add, "I wish that this promise was for me too."

You button up your coat, walk over to the family, and ask if you can ride with them to the city. They agree, and you climb into the back seat of the car.

You look out the back window as the car pulls away and wonder if you'll ever be back.

The End

For another chance to exercise your faith, turn to page 92.

You jump up so quickly that you drop your notebook on the classroom floor. You run into the hallway and look around frantically for anyone you know.

"Kayla, wait up," you hear a voice say to someone behind you. Turning, you recognize Jamey Simon.

"Jamey," you say. "Where's your mom?"

Jamey looks at you quizzically. Your eyes are frantic with worry. Suddenly, Jamey realizes that you don't just need her mom—you need a doctor.

"My mom's either at the hospital or she's at home sleeping," Jamey answers.

You run down the hallway toward the doors and outside.

"Do you need help?" Jamey calls out after you.

18

You don't hear her—you're already on your way to find Dr. Simon.

If you run to the hospital to find Dr. Simon, turn to page 84.

If you run to Jamey's house to find Dr. Simon, turn to page 82.

G racie smiles at you, and you decide to trust her.

"Where are we going?" you ask.

"Hop on back," she says, handing you a helmet.

You put the helmet on and jump on the back of Gracie's scooter. She pushes away, and you hold on tight.

You scoot like this all the way to the café. "What smells so delicious?" you ask Gracie.

Gracie shrugs her shoulders. "Let's find out!" she says.

You follow Gracie through the café and into the kitchen. You both spot what smells so delicious. Gracie hands you one of her mom's famous trail-mix brownies.

You both nibble on the snacks and wander out to the garden.

"Look!" Gracie yells so loudly that you almost drop the brownie.

Turning, you see her. It's Peachie! You watch the moose nibble on her snack—all the plants and flowers in the garden.

"See," Gracie says with a smile. "I knew that you weren't the plant thief."

"If you tell everyone, maybe they'll believe you," you say.

Gracie frowns. "No," she says. "You have to tell them. They'll believe you!"

"Quick," you say, brushing the brownie crumbs off your hands. "We have to go back to the school!"

"Let's scoot!" says Gracie.

Turn to page 86.

Hop in," Stan says, opening the passenger door for you and Natasha.

"Where to?" he asks, backing the truck out of the loading bay.

"Drop me off at the academy," says Natasha, balancing her teacher's planner on her lap.

"How about you?" Stan asks you.

You shrug your shoulders. You don't want to be accused of being a plant thief again.

The truck rumbles past the café. You smell something delicious, and your stomach rumbles. Then you see her! Standing in the middle of Miss Michelle's garden is Peachie! The moose is eating Miss Michelle's plants. The garden is almost empty!

Peachie is the plant-and-flower thief. Or the plant-and-flower eater anyway!

Stan stops the truck in front of the school.

Natasha hops out, but you feel frozen in place.

"What's the matter?" Stan asks.

"I know who the plant thief is," you say. "But what if no one believes me?"

"Do you know the story of the man who was paralyzed by the pool of Bethesda?" Stan asks.

You nod.

"When Jesus told him to rise, what did he do?"

You think back to Chaplain Jake's class. "He took up his bed and walked!"

"Believe Jesus will help you too," Stan says. "Go!"

Turn to page 86.

Hello there," Principal Reeder says. His friendliness makes you feel just a little less nervous. "Now, what's going on?" he adds.

You feel your lower lip tremble. "I didn't mean to," you explain.

"You didn't mean to what?" Principal Reeder asks in a way that makes you want to tell him more.

"I was pulling out my notebook, and I accidentally hit Harold in the throat," you explain.

"I see," Principal Reeder answers. "Is he all right?"

You shrug your shoulders.

"Does he need medical attention?" he asks, reaching for the phone.

"He has medical attention," you answer.

"Well, thank you for telling me what happened. Let's go and see if Harold's OK."

You follow Principal Reeder through his office door and down the hallway. You stare at your shoes as you walk—will anyone believe you that hitting Harold was an accident?

Principal Reeder swings the classroom door open, and you squeeze your eyes closed. You don't want to see what's inside. Will there be blood? Will Harold be on a stretcher? Will his neck be purple?

"There's no one here," Principal Reeder says.

You open your eyes and you see that he's right. There's no Harold and no sign that anything unusual happened in the classroom at all. Walking to the front of the room, Principal Reeder sees your notebook on the floor. He picks it up and hands it to you.

"Sit down," Principal Reeder says, sliding a chair over to you. You feel your hands quiver in your lap as you cling nervously to your notebook.

"I hope that Harold's all right," you say.

Principal Reeder nods. "I'll check on him," he answers. "First, I want to check on you."

Surprised, you ask, "On me?"

"Yes," Principal Reeder adds. "Do you want forgiveness for what happened?"

"It was an accident," you explain. "I don't have

anyone to tell you that's true. There wasn't anyone else here."

"You can stand up now," Principal Reeder says. "I believe you, and I believe that Harold will forgive you."

You stand up and see that the principal's hand is outstretched—he's waiting for you to shake it.

"I can't shake your hand," you answer, surprising yourself. "I need to earn Harold's forgiveness first."

Principal Reeder puts his hand in his pocket. "All right," he says. "How will you do that?"

You shove your notebook into your pocket. "First, I have to find Harold."

"Where will you look?" Principal Reeder asks.

If you think that Harold is badly hurt, look for him at the hospital. Turn to page 69.

If you think that Harold isn't badly hurt, look for him at his house. Turn to page 53.

You wave hello to Chaplain Jake and turn toward Mr. Simon.

"Are you ready for a ride?" he asks.

Your face lights up with excitement. "Blue Birdie?" you ask.

"Come on," Mr. Simon says, and you walk to Little Lake together. You climb into Blue Birdie's copilot seat and put on your headset.

You look out the window as Mr. Simon flies low across the lake and over the town.

"Look down there," Mr. Simon says, pointing toward the summer camp. "No plants or flowers," he explains.

You look. There aren't any plants in front of the cafeteria. Then as you fly over the hospital, you see that the flowers that were along the sidewalk this morning are gone.

"There's our culprit," says Mr. Simon.

You look down, and you see her. She's at the church.

"That proves that I didn't steal the plants and flowers," you say.

"That proof was as easy as ABC," Mr. Simon says.

You remember your notes. You pull out your notebook and turn to the right page. Placing the notebook just past the plane's steering wheel, you ask Mr. Simon your question.

"Jamey said that I could find out what *B* is at Trekkers. Can you take me there?"

Mr. Simon examines your notes. "Hold on to your seat," he says. "Prepare for landing."

Turn to page 79.

P anting, you bend over to catch your breath. The climb up to Hadassah's Observatory was tougher than you imagined it would be.

You walk into the observatory and look up at the sky. Even in the middle of the day, it's beautiful. You imagine it lit up with stars on a clear night.

"There you are," you hear a voice say. You sit still—there's nowhere to hide.

Natasha Simon sits down beside you. There's no use running—you're too tired from the climb. She hands you the brown envelope. "Read it," she says.

You unfold the letter and read the words out loud.

Dear Miss Simon,

Do you remember how last week in history class I accidentally broke your favorite mug?

I ordered you a new one like I promised. It will be here on Monday.

Today a kid hit me in the throat. It really hurt. At first, I was angry, but then I remembered the mug. You forgave me, and so I forgive them. Accidents happen!

Your friend,
Harold Peabody

You pass the letter back to Natasha. "Thank you," you say, and she walks away.

You curl up on the floor of the observatory. You think about Harold forgiving you, and a warm, happy feeling washes over you. Your eyes feel heavy, and soon you drift off to sleep.

When you wake up, you're at home in your bed. The whole thing was a dream. You didn't really get to visit Discovery Mountain after all.

The End

For another chance to exercise your faith
turn back to page 9

J amey pushes the stage door open, and you run behind her and outside.

"My mom will help you," Jamey says.

"OK," you say, but you're confused. "Why do I need to go to the hospital?" you ask.

"You just confessed that you stole the plants and flowers from in front of the school!"

"I meant that I confessed to accidentally hitting Harold," you say.

"Oh," says Jamey. "Did he forgive you?"

You nod.

"You're living First John, chapter one, verse nine," Jamey says with a smile. "Do you have something to write with?"

You pull out your notebook and pen and hand both to her.

You watch as she writes in green ink, "If we

confess our sins, He is faithful and just to forgive us our sins and to cleanse us from all unrighteousness" (1 John 1:9).

"You confessed, and Harold forgave you," she says. "God will forgive you too," she adds.

You smile and reach for your notebook. Jamey holds on to it. *"A, B, C,"* she says, pointing to your note. "I know what that means."

"You do?" you ask.

"A is for *ask.* Matthew, chapter seven, verse seven." She hands you the notebook. "You can find *B* at Trekkers."

You turn toward Trekkers, but then you see Mr. Simon. He's walking in the opposite direction, toward the police station.

If you choose to go to Trekkers,
turn to page 79.

If you choose to follow Mr. Simon,
turn to page 26.

You stare at the brown envelope in Harold's hand and shake your head. "Could I come with you?" you ask.

Harold shrugs his shoulders and opens Blue Birdie's door to talk to Mr. Simon.

"Sure, climb on in," he says.

Mr. Simon hands you a headset and you sit down in the copilot's seat.

"Buckle your seat belt," Mr. Simon says, and Blue Birdie floats away from the dock. As the plane lifts into the air, you turn to talk to Harold. That's when you notice that he isn't with you. Far below, you see him walking to Trekkers, the brown envelope in his hand. Puzzled, you look at Mr. Simon.

"He had an important delivery to make," Mr. Simon explains. "He asked me to fly you home."

You'd dreamed of flying in Blue Birdie, but not

33

like this! Mr. Simon flies right over your home and lands Blue Birdie on the water—just a few steps from your door. Exiting the plane, you realize you might never visit Discovery Mountain again. And you'll never know if Harold forgave you.

The End

For another chance to exercise your faith, turn back to page 38.

Ignoring the delicious smell and your rumbling stomach, you walk out of the café. Turning right at the corner, someone nearly crashes into you!

"I didn't see you there," a girl says, straightening her glasses.

"It's okay, Gracie," you say with a smile.

She looks at you quizzically, trying to figure out if she knows you. "I'm sorry that I almost ran into you," she finally says.

"Accidents happen," you answer. Then, you have an idea! Gracie can help you find the right words to prove to Harold that hitting him was an accident.

You take out your notebook and multicolored pen.

"I forgive you," you say. "But if I didn't, how would you convince me to?"

"I can't convince you to forgive me," Gracie says. "Jesus puts forgiveness in your heart."

You write her words down in your notebook. You underline the word "heart."

"What are you writing down?" Gracie asks.

You close your notebook and don't answer her question. "I'm looking for Harold," you say.

"Oh, I heard that he got hurt this morning," Gracie says. "He went to the hospital," she adds.

You turn toward the hospital.

"But Lana said that she saw him going to the church."

If you choose to look for Harold at the hospital, turn to page 69.

If you choose to look for Harold at the church, turn to page 61.

Y ou run to the back of the stage. You grab your flashlight out of your coat pocket, and then you flip the light switch. The lights flicker for a moment and then go out.

You shine your flashlight across the darkened stage. Suddenly, the lights all turn back on!

"There goes the plant thief!" someone yells.

You run for the stairs. You don't notice your notebook slide out of your pocket and fall on the floor behind you.

You slip into a closet and close the door. Sitting on the floor, you lean against the door.

You breathe deeply. Did anyone follow you?

"Pray," you whisper to yourself. "What did Kayla mean?"

You reach for your Bible and look for a verse you underlined last year. You find it. "Therefore I say to you, whatever things you ask when you pray, believe that you receive them, and you will have them" (Mark 11:24).

Silently, you talk to God. You pray about accidentally hitting Harold and about the plant situation. You ask for God's forgiveness.

You read the verse again. "Belief" starts with the letter B. You reach for your notebook, but it isn't in your pocket!

You hear something slide under the door—it's your notebook! There's a note with it.

"I know that you didn't steal the plants. Meet me at Trekkers, and I'll show you."

You read the note again. Who wrote it? Can you trust them, or is it a trap?

If you choose to meet the note writer at Trekkers, turn to page 79.

If you choose to stay in the closet, turn to page 75.

You still haven't found Harold, but you haven't given up. The wind is cool, so you take your hat out of your coat pocket. You feel a little warmer now. You step determinedly. You have to do *something* to convince Harold to forgive you. First, you have to find him. Where is he?

You hear a familiar voice call out. "Harold! Harold!" It sounds like Mr. Simon's voice. You spot him.

Mr. Simon is on the dock on Little Lake, next to Blue Birdie. You run toward him, looking for Harold.

"Harold," Mr. Simon says to you and then realizes his mistake. "Oh, with that hat on, I thought that you were Harold!"

"Mr. Simon, I'm looking for him too," you say, almost out of breath. "Is he here?"

"He's supposed to be," Mr. Simon says. "There he is!"

You turn to see Harold running along the dock toward you. You hear Mr. Simon climb into Blue Birdie and start the plane's engine.

"Come on, Harold, it's time to go," Mr. Simon calls down.

You want to get on the plane with them. This could be your chance to convince Harold to forgive you.

"Hey," Harold says, running past you. "This needs to go to Trekkers. Will you deliver it for me?"

If you choose to deliver the item to Trekkers for Harold, turn to page 40.

If you choose to follow them and climb on Blue Birdie, turn to page 32.

ou reach for the brown envelope that Harold holds out to you. He turns to climb onto Blue Birdie.

You call out after him, "Harold, are you all right? It was an accident!"

The sounds of the wind and Blue Birdie's engine drown out your question. Harold doesn't hear you. You stand on the dock and watch as the plane glides across Little Lake and then lifts off up into the air.

Turning the envelope over in your hands, you read the name on the front.

You walk into Trekkers.

"How may I help you?" a friendly voice asks. For a moment, you forget about your problem with Harold and smile at Natasha Simon.

"Harold asked me to deliver this," you say.

"It's addressed to me," Natasha says. You watch

as she opens the envelope, reads the letter inside, and smiles.

"Well, maybe Harold will forgive me now that I did this favor for him," you mumble, turning to leave.

"Wait!" Natasha calls out. "Are you the kid that hit Harold in the throat?"

Pulling your hat down low, you run for the door. "It was an accident!" you say over your shoulder. What will you do now? You've been recognized as the kid who hurt Harold.

If you choose to run back to the classroom to lay low, turn to page 92.

If you choose to run up to Hadassah's Observatory to hide, turn to page 28.

The worker at the information desk scowls at you.

You show her the candy bar you bought in the gift shop. "Delivery," you say and put on your friendliest smile.

She frowns but waves you through.

You turn left and walk down the hospital corridor. You walk for a while but can't find room 141. You stop a nurse walking past you.

"Excuse me," you ask. "Which way is room one forty-one?"

She points toward the other corridor and then asks you a question. "Are you Harold's grandchild?"

You laugh, and then you realize something. Room 141 can't be Harold Peabody's room. He isn't old enough to have grandchildren.

"I'm looking for Harold Peabody," you tell the nurse.

"Oh," she answers with a giggle. "He was here earlier, but he's been discharged."

You ask the nurse where Harold went.

"Oh, he left with his dad," she says. "I imagine he went home. Or perhaps to the church."

Putting the candy bar in your pocket, you're glad that you didn't spend all your money on a bouquet after all. You walk out of the hospital to keep looking for Harold.

If you choose to look for him at his house, turn to page 53.

If you choose to look for him at the church, turn to page 61.

You step through the door, and the sound of a noisy crowd hits you.

"This way," Principal Reeder says. You walk past a long curtain, and your foot catches in the fabric. Tripping, you fall forward.

The sound of laughter washes over you. You blink into the bright lights. You're standing on the gym stage in front of a school assembly.

"Are you all right?" Principal Reeder asks and helps you to stand up.

Your cheeks feel hot with embarrassment. "I'm all right," you whisper.

Principal Reeder reaches for the microphone. It squeals, and the crowd quiets. "Let's all welcome our visitor," he says.

You wish that you could fall through a hole in the stage floor and disappear.

45

"I called you all here," Principal Reeder says in a serious voice, "because all of the flowers and plants in front of the school are missing. Has anyone," he asks, "seen or heard anything new or unusual today?"

Every eye in the gym turns to you. You remember Kayla's advice and reach for the microphone.

"Let's pray that the thief is caught," you say.

You look back at Kayla. She shakes her head. That wasn't what she meant by "pray."

Frantic, you look for a way to escape. On the wall behind Kayla, you see a light switch and a lever.

If you choose to flip the light switch, turn to page 36.

If you choose to hit the lever, turn to page 73.

N ervously, you step inside Pastor Peabody's office. He closes the door, and as you turn, you see Harold.

"Harold," you say quickly. "It was an accident. I'm so sorry!"

You can't take your eyes off of Harold. Is he all right? Is he angry? "Are you all right?" you ask.

"I'm OK now," Harold answers. "But it was a little tough to talk for a few hours."

"It was an accident," you repeat.

Pastor Peabody hands you a piece of paper. "This is what we wanted to show you," he says.

You read a letter written by Harold to Natasha Simon. You smile and hand it back. Harold folds it and puts it in a brown envelope.

"She forgave you, so you forgive me," you say.

Harold smiles. "Accidents happen!"

"God forgives all of us," Pastor Peabody adds. " 'There is therefore now no condemnation to those who are in Christ Jesus, who do not walk according to the flesh, but according to the Spirit.' That's Romans, chapter eight, verse one."

"Time to get back to school," Pastor Peabody says to Harold.

Turning to you, he adds, "Do you need a ride home?"

Nodding, you agree. Harold and Logan jump into the car to go with you. You have your answer—Harold forgives you. But, riding home, you feel as though you're missing something. You feel like you were supposed to learn more while on this faith exercise.

The End

For another chance to exercise your faith, turn back to page 61.

You take a deep breath and turn around.

Meow!

"Stormy!" you say, relieved to see the cat. You reach out to pet her, but Stormy runs from you.

You laugh and run after her. Turning the corner quickly, you walk right into the flower bed. It used to be the flower bed anyway—the flowers are virtually all gone.

You hear a noise at the edge of the woods. Turning, you see her.

Meow!

"See, Stormy," you say, pointing to the woods. "I didn't steal the plants. She did!"

Stormy runs through the churchyard. You chase after her. You step on a rock and slip and twist your ankle as you land.

"Are you all right?" a voice asks.

You hold your ankle and blink back a tear. "No," you whimper.

"Can I call someone for you?" Pastor Peabody asks.

You give him a phone number. He dials and then helps you hobble back to the church steps. Your ankle really hurts. A car pulls up, and Pastor Peabody helps you inside. On your drive down the mountain, you feel your ankle throb with pain. And that isn't the worst thing. Frantic, you check your coat pocket. You forgot your notebook on the church steps. Will you ever see it again?

The End

For another chance to exercise your faith, turn to page 73.

You reach for Lana's left hand. She hands you a colorful bookmark. "Discovery Mountain: The Trail Mix Capital of the West," you read.

"Thank you, Lana," you say with a laugh. You reach into your pocket and pull out your notebook. Carefully, you tuck the bookmark inside.

"If you lose it, you'll have to come back for another one someday," Principal Reeder says.

"Thank you for the bookmark and the faith exercise," you say to Principal Reeder.

The crowd of students and teachers rushes up onto the stage. Everyone wants to talk to you!

"Welcome to Discovery Mountain," they say. You thank them, but you think that they should be saying goodbye instead—your faith exercise is almost over.

The crowd feels suffocating.

"*Psst*," a voice says. It's Logan.

"Follow me," he says, and he leads you away from the crowd and to the back of the stage.

"Someone's waiting to talk to you," Logan explains and waves goodbye.

It's Harold!

You flip the pages in your notebook. "I still don't know what C is," you tell him.

"Sure, you do," Harold says. "You just did C."

You have no idea what he's talking about.

"Give me your pen," Harold says.

You hand him your pen and notebook. Next to your letter C, Harold writes, "John 11:41. Jesus said, 'Father, I thank You that You have heard Me.' "

You don't understand.

"C is for *claim*," Harold explains. "First, you *ask* God for His forgiveness. Next you *believe* that He gives it. Then you *claim* the promise for yourself. God hears you—just like He listened to Jesus in John, chapter eleven, verse forty-one."

"Just like Jesus healed the paralyzed man," you add. "He heals my heart. Because He promised, I believe it."

Harold hands you your notebook. He holds on to the pen, clicking through the colors.

"This is a cool pen," he says.

"Keep it," you say. "I have another one at home."

Harold puts the pen in his pocket and smiles. "So this is goodbye."

"Until I find my way back," you say with a wave.

You walk down the hall and outside. Passing Trekkers, you walk onto the dock and out onto Little Lake. Someone's inside Blue Birdie.

"Do you need a lift somewhere?" Chaplain Jake asks, yelling over the sound of the plane's engine.

"Come on in," Kayla says.

You climb into the seat behind Kayla and put on your headset.

"Chaplain Jake," you ask, "how did you end up in Discovery Mountain?"

"God brought me here!" he answers with a big grin. "God sends just the right people to Discovery Mountain."

Blue Birdie floats out onto Little Lake and lifts into the air. You watch the town get smaller and smaller below you. You hope you'll find your way back here again—someday.

The End

To begin your faith exercise again, turn to page 9.

You button up your coat as you walk away from Discovery Mountain Academy. You think about what you can say to convince Harold to forgive you. You try to think of the perfect argument to prove to him that it was an accident.

You reach the corner—something smells delicious! You turn to your right and then to your left. You don't know which way to turn to get to Harold's house. You step inside Miss Michelle's Café to ask for directions.

"Welcome to the café," a familiar voice says. It's Miss Michelle!

"Is that your famous potato leek soup that I smell?" you ask.

"Yes, are you hungry?" Miss Michelle asks and motions to an open spot at the counter.

You remember to ask for directions to Harold's house.

"Just turn right at the corner," Miss Michelle answers.

You thank her and turn to leave.

"Wouldn't you like some soup before you go?" Miss Michelle asks.

You could use a little more time to work on your argument. And, besides, the soup smells delicious!

If you choose to stay at the café and have lunch, turn to page 71.

If you choose to keep walking to Harold's house, turn to page 34.

You follow Chaplain Jake out into the hallway. Instead of turning to the right to Principal Reeder's office, he turns to the left.

"Where are we going?" you ask.

"Oh, this is big news," Chaplain Jake says and turns toward the school gym.

You hear students talking in the gym. It sounds like a large group, and just as you wonder if Chaplain Jake is leading you into a school assembly, he turns the other direction.

Jamey and Kayla stand outside of a closed door at the end of the hallway. Chaplain Jake runs ahead of you and slips behind the door.

"They found you," Kayla says as you approach.

"What's going on?" you ask her.

"It's a surprise," Jamey says, but she isn't smiling.

Kayla reaches for the door handle. "You could always pray," she says to you.

"Or you could confess," Jamey adds.

Kayla opens the door and motions for you to step through.

If you choose to follow Kayla's advice, turn to page 44.

If you choose to follow Jamey's advice, turn to page 59.

If you choose to try to escape, turn to page 15.

Y ou shove your notebook back in your pocket, pull out your wide-brimmed hat, and cover your face. You sneak into the hallway. With your head down, you walk toward the doors. You did it! You left the school without anyone seeing you. No one knows that it was you who accidentally hit Harold. You run as quickly as you can to the bus station. Climbing on the bus, you feel relieved. But then you start to worry. Is Harold all right? And what about your questions about John 5? Will you ever find the answers? When the bus slows to a stop, you walk up to the driver.

"Excuse me, can I get off the bus and go back to Discovery Mountain?"

The driver looks at you, confused. "Discovery Mountain?" he asks. "Where is that?"

"That's where I was when I got on the bus," you answer.

"You've been reading too many storybooks," the driver answers and shakes his head.

You walk back to your seat, and then you realize what's happened. That was your only chance to visit Discovery Mountain. That was your only chance to exercise your faith. You ride home—disappointed.

The End

For another chance to exercise your faith, turn back to page 9.

Y ou step through the door, and the sound of a noisy crowd hits you.

"This way," Principal Reeder says. You follow him past a long curtain and into the light.

You hear a microphone squeal, and the crowd quiets. You blink into the bright lights. You're standing on the gym stage in front of a school assembly.

"I called you all here," Principal Reeder says, "because all of the flowers and plants in front of the school are missing."

You take a small step backward. Maybe it isn't too late to escape.

"Has anyone seen or heard anything new or unusual today?" Principal Reeder asks.

You freeze in place as every eye in the gym turns to you.

"Oh," Principal Reeder says with a laugh. "We

want to welcome our visitor too!"

Your cheeks flush red with embarrassment as the crowd claps to welcome you.

Principal Reeder hands you the microphone.

As your hands shake nervously, you blurt out, "I confess."

Everyone begins to talk at once. You hear someone shout, "Plant stealer!"

"You confess?" Principal Reeder asks.

"To accidentally hitting Harold," you explain and turn to run away.

"Quick, follow me," says Kayla.

"No! I'll take you to the hospital," says Jamey.

If you choose to follow Kayla,
turn to page 63.

If you choose to follow Jamey,
turn to page 30.

Your stomach rumbles. You reach into your coat pocket and unwrap the candy bar. It isn't a balanced lunch, but it quiets your stomach.

Walking up the hill to Harmony Corner church, you wonder what Harold told his dad, Pastor Peabody, about what happened. *Will they both be angry at you?* After walking up the church steps, you knock. The door opens by itself. Stepping inside, you hear voices, but you don't see anyone. *Maybe you should say a few prayers*, you think. Maybe if you pray hard enough, Harold will forgive you.

"Hey, it's you!" You jump, startled by the sudden whisper. You see that it's Logan Lewis.

"What are you doing here?" you ask.

"I volunteer here," Logan answers. "Hey, you're the one who hit Harold, aren't you?"

You jump up, ready to run.

"It's all right," Logan says. "It was an accident, wasn't it?"

You nod.

"Come on, I want to show you something," he says and walks down the stairs.

You hesitate, wondering if you can trust him. At that moment, a door swings open.

"Ah, it's you," a voice says.

You turn to see Pastor Peabody standing outside his now-open office door. "Come in. I want to show you something," he says.

If you choose to follow Logan,
turn to page 77.

If you choose to follow Pastor Peabody,
turn to page 46.

Kayla pushes the stage door open, and you run behind her and outside.

"The police station is there," she points and adds, "Do you have something to write with?"

You pull out your notebook and pen and hand both to her.

"Show my dad this," she says, scribbling something on the page.

You thank her and run to the police station. Bursting into the lobby, you nearly run into Officer Lewis.

"May I help you?" he asks, looking down at you.

You're too afraid to speak! You show him the note from Kayla.

Without saying a word, Officer Lewis steps inside a small side room. You follow him and sit at the table. He writes something on the whiteboard.

You copy the words down in your notebook. "If we confess our sins, He is faithful and just to forgive us our sins and to cleanse us from all unrighteousness" (1 John 1:9).

Officer Lewis leans across the table. "I know a little something about confessions," he says.

You shrink into the chair.

"I know that you didn't steal the plants," he says.

"Oh?" you squeak.

"Step outside. Mr. Simon and Chaplain Jake will show you why."

You walk outside where they are waiting for you.

If you choose to go with Chaplain Jake, turn to page 67.

If you choose to go with Mr. Simon, turn to page 26.

A *choo!* The flowers in the bouquet tickle your nose. You hold on to the glass vase tightly and stifle another sneeze. You turn right and walk down the hospital corridor. Reading the room numbers, you stop just outside of room 141.

"Harold, take your medication, and you'll feel better," you hear the nurse say.

You wait for the nurse to leave the room. "Delivery!" you say as cheerfully as your nerves will let you.

"Come in," a voice croaks.

You walk to the edge of the bed, the flowers in front of you. Setting them down, you look down at the bed.

"You're not Harold!" you holler.

The older man looks at you, confused. "I'm Harold—Harold Anderson."

You pick up the flowers.

"Thank you for the flowers," the other Harold says. "They brighten up my whole room."

You don't have the heart to take the flowers away. You set them back down, smile, and walk back into the corridor.

You bought the best bouquet in the gift shop. You thought that you could buy Harold's forgiveness.

You're out of money. Now what will you do?

If you choose to look somewhere else for Harold, turn to page 38.

If you choose to give up and go back to the classroom, turn to page 92.

Y ou wave hello to Mr. Simon and turn toward Chaplain Jake.

"You can prove that I didn't steal the flowers and plants?" you ask.

"Are you hungry?" Chaplain Jake asks.

"Not really," you answer. Chaplain Jake ignores your answer and walks toward the café. You follow.

"Miss Michelle made her famous trail-mix brownies," Chaplain Jake says.

You start to tell him that you're not hungry, but Chaplain Jake puts his fingers to his lips. "*Shhhh*," he whispers. "You'll scare her away."

You look past the café to the garden and smile. "That proves that I didn't steal the plants and flowers," you say.

Chaplain Jake runs up the stairs to the café. You start to follow, but you notice something else in the garden. It's a hot-air balloon!

Stepping inside the hot-air balloon basket, you feel it rise from the ground. You look out at the ground below. Discovery Mountain looks smaller and smaller. You strain your eyes, but you can't see the town anymore. Were you really just there, or did you imagine the whole thing?

The End

For another chance to exercise your faith, turn back to page 63.

You burst into the hospital lobby. The worker at the information desk looks over the top of her glasses at you.

"Yes?" she asks.

You aren't convinced that she wants to help you, but you ask your question anyway.

"Is Harold Peabody here?"

She glances down at the list of patients on the paper in front of her.

"Are you a family member?" she asks.

You shake your head. You try to read her list.

"Are you delivering something?" she adds.

You shake your head no again. Looking at the list of patient names, you read, "Harold, room 141."

She notices you looking at the list and turns the paper upside down. "If you're not delivering something and you're not a family member, I can't help you," she says coolly.

You turn away and think about running past the desk and up the stairs to room 141, but the worker is watching you closely.

Then you notice the gift shop. You have an idea! You'll buy Harold something, and the woman at the desk will have to let you past to deliver it to his room.

Reaching for your wallet, you walk into the gift shop.

If you buy the biggest bouquet in the gift shop, turn to page 65.

If you buy the least expensive thing in the gift shop, turn to page 42.

You take the empty seat at the café counter.

"One order of potato leek soup," Miss Michelle says, setting the steaming bowl in front of you.

"Anything else?" Miss Michelle asks.

You realize that this might be your only chance to eat at Miss Michelle's Café. You order a sandwich and an Apple Day bar for dessert.

Enjoying the delicious food, you take out your notebook. You write these words down in a list:

- *accident*
- *convince*
- *argument*
- *win*
- *forgive*

Finishing your Apple Day bar, you stuff your notebook back into your coat pocket. Miss Michelle hands you the bill for your meal, and you have just enough money left to pay it.

Stepping outside, you feel sleepy. And you still haven't thought of the perfect argument to convince Harold to forgive you. You stand at the corner and look to the right and then the left.

If you choose to turn right, toward Harold's house, turn to page 38.

If you choose to turn left and go back to the academy to take a nap, turn to page 92.

Y ou run to the back of the stage. You look at the pulley system connected to the lever and take a risk. You pull the lever and turn. As you expect, the heavy stage curtain automatically closes.

You run across the stage, carefully staying hidden behind the closing curtain. You run down the stairs.

"Plant thief!" a voice hollers.

You run through the door and outside before anyone else can spot you.

Kayla's words run through your mind. "You could always pray!" You keep walking until you look up and realize you're standing on the front steps of the church.

Well, this is a good place to pray, you think as you sit down. You hear a fluttering sound and reach down to pick up the piece of paper. It's last week's church bulletin. You read the verse on the front. "Therefore I say to you, whatever things you ask when you pray, believe that you receive them, and you will have them" (Mark 11:24).

The verse is familiar. You reach for your notebook and tuck the bulletin inside. You study the verse. You write "Believe?" next to the letter *B* in your note from earlier.

You feel something brush against your back. Startled, you jump to your feet! What could it be? Do you dare look?

If you choose to turn and look,
turn to page 48.

If you run back to the safety of the school,
turn to page 75.

Y ou check that the closet door is closed tightly and lean against it. You feel safe here in the school closet. You turn your notebook over in your hands and think about the verse you just read in Mark 11.

You close your eyes and whisper a prayer. "Lord, You say that whatever I ask when I pray that I should believe that You will answer. I want to believe, Lord. Please show me how."

You hear a noise outside the closet door—it's getting louder, and it sounds familiar. So you close your eyes and listen carefully. *Could it be?* you wonder.

Did someone follow you here?

The noise gets louder and then stops right outside the door. You move quietly away from the door. Mustering all of your courage, you place your hand on the doorknob. You take a deep breath and throw the door wide open.

Bark! Bark!

"Gadget," you say and bend down to hug him. "I hoped it was you! Come on, boy, let's go for a walk!"

Take a walk to Trekkers.

Turn to page 79.

You explain to Pastor Peabody that Logan is expecting you to follow him. Disappointed, Pastor Peabody closes his office door.

You walk down the stairs and look for Logan. Where did he go?

"Look at this," Logan says, again startling you!

You frown a little because he scared you, and then you turn and look where he's pointing. You read the verse painted in cursive letters on the wall. " 'For God so loved the world that He gave His only begotten Son, that whoever believes in Him should not perish but have everlasting life,' John, chapter three, verse sixteen."

"Whenever I'm not sure of what to do, I read that verse," Logan says.

You take out your notebook and write down the reference: "John 3:16." You want to read it again later.

You wonder if God so loves the world, can God forgive you, even if Harold can't?

Outside you hear sirens. You freeze in place. *What's wrong? Why are the police here?*

"Oh, my dad's here to take me back to school," Logan explains. "Come on; we'll give you a ride."

You freeze in place. Officer Lewis could be here to give his son a ride. Or could he could be looking for you? You wonder where you can hide.

If you choose to accept a ride back to the school with Logan and Officer Lewis, turn to page 92.

If you choose to run up to Hadassah's Observatory to hide, turn to page 28.

You push open the doors to Trekkers and walk across the wooden floor.

Bark! Bark!

"Come here, Gadget," you say and scratch him behind the ear. "Where do I find the answer? What is *B*?"

"Did you say *B*?" a voice asks.

Natasha is dusting the shelf behind you.

You reach for your notebook and turn to the page with your notes. "Is *B* for *believe*?"

"Come with me," Natasha answers. You follow her through Trekkers and out to the loading bay.

"Look!" she says, pointing to the wall behind you. You turn and read.

"*Believe*. 'For God so loved the world that He gave His only begotten Son, that whoever *believes*

in Him should not perish but have everlasting life
(John 3:16).' "

"My favorite verse," Natasha explains. "I painted
it here—and at the church too."

You remember seeing this verse before. You flip
back through your notebook. Yes, there it is.

You click your pen to the black-colored ink. Next
to the *B*, you write, "Believe. Mark 11:24. John
3:16."

"Are you on a faith exercise?" Natasha asks,
watching you write.

"Yes," you answer. "How did you know?" you add,
clicking your pen and closing your notebook.

"Oh," Natasha says with a knowing smile.
"You're not the first person I've shown this wall to."

You hear—and feel—a loud rumble.
Instinctively, you grab Natasha's arm to steady
yourself.

"It's not an earthquake," she laughs. "That's the
loading bay door opening."

You turn and watch the heavy metal door slide
up—the lights of a big truck flood into the loading
bay. The truck rolls inside, and you see the driver's
door open. You run to greet him.

"Stan!" you say.

Your enthusiasm startles him. He looks past

you to Natasha. "Faith exerciser," you hear her say.

Stan nods. "I'll give you and Natasha a ride in the truck after I finish my deliveries," he says. "If you'd like it."

"I'd love that!" you say. You feel so happy that you forget about being accused of being a thief.

"There you are!" a voice calls out.

Suddenly you remember. You run through the open loading bay door—straight into her.

"There you are," Gracie says again, one foot on her scooter and the other on the ground.

You blink your eyes. Is Gracie here to help you or to accuse you of being a plant thief? You can't tell.

"Did you get my note?" she asks.

You don't answer.

"Well, come on," she says. "I'll show you."

If you choose to ride in the truck with Stan and Natasha, turn to page 21.

If you choose to go with Gracie, turn to page 19.

You run up the steps, but as you reach out to knock on the door, you hesitate. You wonder if you have found the right house. Then you hear a familiar sound. *Bark! Bark!*

"Gadget," you say through the closed door. "Go and wake up Dr. Simon."

You hear Gadget run back through the house. Not sure if he understood you, you knock on the door anyway. Standing on the doorstep, you think about Harold. Maybe Dr. Simon is at the hospital. You're standing here, wasting time when Harold could hardly breathe! Just as you turn to leave, you hear the door handle turn.

"Oh, hello," Dr. Simon says with a yawn.

"Dr. Simon," you start to say, but you feel terrible for waking her up.

"Is this a medical emergency?" Dr. Simon asks,

seeing your concerned face. "I worked last night; you should go to the hospital."

Gadget barks at you—it's like he wants you to tell Dr. Simon everything. You bend down to scratch Gadget behind his ear, and you decide to blurt out everything that happened.

Grabbing her car keys, Dr. Simon runs to her car. "Come on, let's get to the school quickly," she says. "I'll check on Harold. Go and tell Principal Reeder what happened!"

Your heart seems to skip a beat as you walk to the principal's office. You hit one of his students, but it was an accident. Will he believe you?

Turn to page 23.

You run up the sidewalk toward the hospital. The glass doors open automatically, and you burst into the front lobby, your hair a mess, panting for breath. The worker at the information desk looks over the top of her glasses at you. "How may I help you?" she asks calmly.

"I need to see Dr. Simon," you say, brushing sweat off your forehead.

"Dr. Simon is off today," she answers, unmoved by your frantic state. "Is this a medical emergency?" she asks.

"It is!" you answer.

She points you in the direction of the nurse's station.

"May I help you?" a soothing voice asks. It's Nurse Megan. Hearing her familiar voice, you blurt out everything that happened.

85

Without even grabbing her coat, Nurse Megan runs ahead of you and out the hospital door. "I'll check on Harold," she calls back to you. "Go tell Principal Reeder what happened!"

You try to keep up with her as you run back to the academy. You shudder as you think about telling the principal that you hit one of his students—even if it was an accident. Will he believe you?

Turn to page 23.

T hank you for the ride," you call out behind you. You burst through the front doors of the academy. There's no one in the hallway. *Where is everyone?* you wonder.

"It's you!" a voice calls.

You start to run, but then you stop—so quickly that you nearly fall forward. You remember that you don't have to run anymore. Turning, you see Harold running up behind you.

"I'm not the plant thief," you say confidently.

"I know. We know," Harold says. "Come on. Everyone's waiting."

You wonder what they're waiting for, but you go with Harold. You walk through the empty halls and the gym doors.

Harold walks straight up the center aisle of the crowded gym. Everyone is still in the assembly.

"Harold, you found our visitor," Principal Reeder says into the microphone. "Come up on stage!"

Your knees tremble. Gracie smiles at you encouragingly from across the gym.

"Come on," Harold whispers. "I'll go with you."

Your heart beats faster as you walk onto the stage.

"We thought that you left," Principal Reeder says.

You shake your head.

"A few of us," Principal Reeder says, looking out at the crowded gym, "accused you of being a plant-and-flower thief."

Your lip quivers.

"You aren't a plant-and-flower thief," Principal Reeder says apologetically. "It turns out that Peachie, the moose, was just very, very hungry this morning."

A nervous laugh ripples through the gym.

Principal Reeder stretches out his hand to you—he's waiting for you to shake it. "Will you forgive us?" he asks.

You look at his outstretched hand, and time seems to freeze. You think about the miracle of Jesus healing the paralyzed man. The man believed that Jesus would heal him, and he stood up and walked.

You asked God to forgive you. Do you believe that He has? Slowly, you reach out and shake Principal Reeder's hand.

Everyone cheers!

Gathering your courage, you reach for the microphone.

"I forgive you," you say. "Do you know what's worse than being paralyzed with no one to help you for thirty-eight years? Not being forgiven. I forgive you because Harold forgave me," you say, smiling over at him. "And God forgave me too," you add.

You hand the microphone to Principal Reeder and turn to run off the stage.

"Wait," Principal Reeder calls out. You turn around and see Lana standing beside Principal Reeder. She has something in each hand, and she's holding them out to you.

"We have a small welcome gift for you," Principal Reeder says.

You look at the gifts in Lana's outstretched hands. Will you accept one?

If you choose to accept the gift in Lana's right hand, turn to page 89.

If you choose to accept the gift in Lana's left hand, turn to page 50.

You reach for Lana's right hand. She hands you a colorful sticker. "Discovery Mountain: Where God sends just the right people," you read.

"Thank you, Lana," you say as you reach into your pocket and pull out your notebook. Carefully, you place the sticker on the cover.

"That looks pretty nice there," Principal Reeder says, admiring your sticker placement.

"Thank you—for the sticker and the faith exercise," you say to Principal Reeder.

The crowd of students and teachers rushes up onto the stage. Everyone wants to talk to you!

"Welcome to Discovery Mountain," they say. You thank them, but you think that they should be saying goodbye instead—your faith exercise is almost over.

The crowd feels suffocating. You feel a hand grab your arm, and someone pulls you away from the crowd.

"Chaplain Jake!" you exclaim.

"I don't like crowds either," he explains.

"Chaplain Jake," you ask, "how did you end up in Discovery Mountain?"

"God brought me here!" he answers with a big grin. "Look—someone's waiting to talk to you."

Harold motions to you from the back of the stage, and you run over to him.

You flip the pages in your notebook. "I still don't know what *C* is," you say.

"Sure you do," Harold says. "You just did *C*."

You have no idea what he's talking about.

"Give me your pen," Harold says.

You hand him your pen and notebook. Next to your letter *C*, Harold writes, "John 11:41. Jesus said 'Father, I thank You that You have heard Me.' "

You don't understand.

"*C* is for *claim*," Harold explains. "First, you *ask* God for His forgiveness. Next you *believe* that He gives it. Then you *claim* the promise for yourself. God hears you—just like He listened to Jesus in John, chapter eleven, verse forty-one."

"Just like Jesus healed the paralyzed man," you

add. "He heals my heart. Because He promised, I believe it."

Harold hands you your notebook. Turning to the back page, you scribble something down, tear out the page, and hand it to him.

"What's this?" Harold asks.

"My address. Visit me if you're ever in my area."

Harold puts the paper in his pocket and smiles. "So this is goodbye."

"Until I find my way back," you say with a wave.

You walk out the door, down the hall, and outside.

A big truck rumbles past, and the brakes screech as it stops next to you.

"Do you need a ride somewhere?" Stan asks.

Bark! Bark!

"Come on. We'll give you a lift," Jamey says.

You climb into the passenger seat next to Jamey, and Gadget climbs onto your lap, eagerly waiting for you to scratch him behind his ears. You hope you'll find your way back here again—someday.

The End

To begin your faith exercise again, turn to page 9.

You push one of the desks into a quiet corner in Chaplain Jake's classroom. You almost can't believe everything that's happened. "Is this a dream?" you wonder out loud.

You pull your notebook and multicolored pen out of your coat pocket. Flipping through the pages, you see that you only have pieces of information. You don't have any answers.

You take your Bible out of your other pocket and open it to John. You run your finger over the heart you drew earlier. You read the verse again. "Rise, take up your bed, and walk." Your eye lands on two words that you underlined further down the page: "worse thing."

You click your pen to the blue ink color and write "John 5:14" in your notebook. Underneath you write, "What could be worse than being paralyzed with no one to help you for thirty-eight years?"

You try to remember what Chaplain Jake said earlier. You write, "Forgiveness of sin?" next to your question.

You're deep in thought when you feel a finger tap you on the shoulder. Jumping to your feet, you swing around to look behind you.

"Hey, don't hit me again," Harold laughs.

You reach for your things and plan to run for the door.

Harold sets his hand on your notebook. "Please don't run away," he says.

You stare at his face for a moment. He's smiling. You stand up straight and look him in the eye. "Harold," you ask, "do you forgive me?"

Harold sits down in your seat. "Of course, accidents happen!" he says.

You want to believe him. But you have questions.

"It's like John five," Harold says, pointing to your open page. "Jesus asked the paralyzed man if he wanted to be made well."

You listen.

"Jesus told the man to stand up and walk. All the man had to do was listen to Jesus," Harold says and picks up your multicolored pen. He clicks it repeatedly. You find the sound annoying, but you don't tell him that.

"Harold," you ask, "Why do you forgive me? Really?"

"Simple ABCs," he answers, still clicking.

You look at him, confused.

"God forgives me when I ask Him. *A* is for *ask*: Matthew, chapter seven, verse seven, '*Ask*, and it will be given to you; seek, and you will find; knock, and it will be opened to you.'"

You reach for your notebook, and he hands you your pen.

"There you are!"

You and Harold both jump at the sound of Chaplain Jake's voice.

"Come on," Chaplain Jake says. "Principal Reeder found something, and he wants to see you!"

"Me?" Harold asks.

"No," Chaplain Jake answers and looks your way. "You!" he says.

Quickly you scribble "A, B, C" in your notebook.

"Well, what are you waiting for?" Chaplain Jake asks.

If you choose to follow Chaplain Jake, turn to page 55.

If you choose to try to escape, turn to page 15.

Faith Exercise Notes

Keep track of the Bible verses and the important things that you learn during your faith exercise.